BENTLY & egg

Story and Pictures by

WILLIAM JOYCE

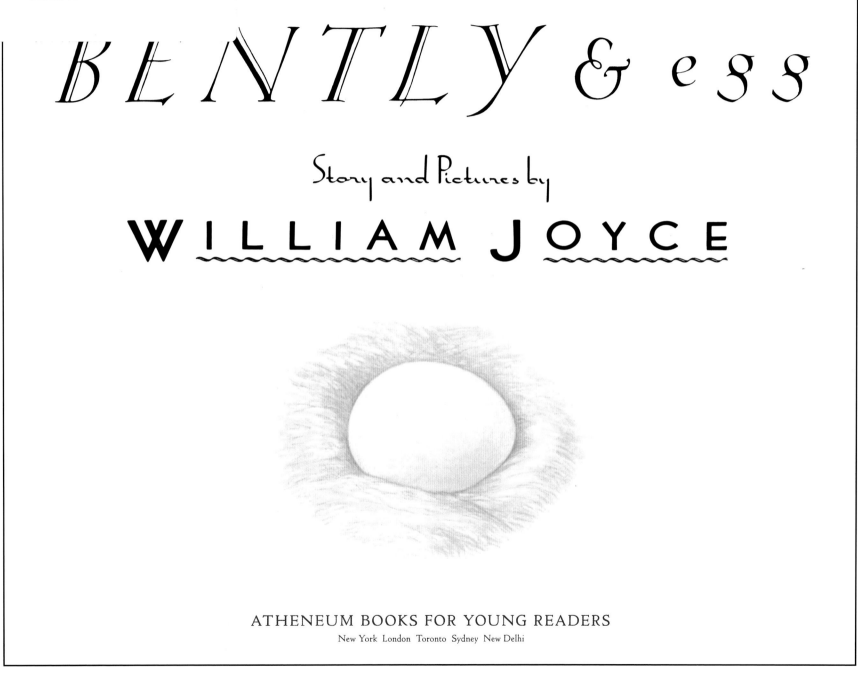

ATHENEUM BOOKS FOR YOUNG READERS

New York London Toronto Sydney New Delhi

ATHENEUM BOOKS FOR YOUNG READERS • An imprint of Simon & Schuster Children's Publishing Division • 1230 Avenue of the Americas, New York, New York 10020 • Copyright © 1992 by William Joyce • Originally published in 1992 by Laura Geringer Books/HarperCollins Publishers • All rights reserved, including the right of reproduction in whole or in part in any form. • ATHENEUM BOOKS FOR YOUNG READERS is a registered trademark of Simon & Schuster, Inc. • Atheneum logo is a trademark of Simon & Schuster, Inc. • For information about special discounts for bulk purchases, please contact Simon & Schuster Special Sales at 1-866-506-1949 or business@simonandschuster.com. • The Simon & Schuster Speakers Bureau can bring authors to your live event. For more information or to book an event, contact the Simon & Schuster Speakers Bureau at 1-866-248-3049 or visit our website at www.simonspeakers.com. • Book design by Alicia Mikles, based on an original design by Christine Kettner. • The text for this book was set in Cg Cloister. • The illustrations for this book were rendered in acrylic. • Manufactured in China • 0117 SCP • First Atheneum Books for Young Readers Edition • 10 9 8 7 6 5 4 3 2 1 • CIP data for this book is available from the Library of Congress. • ISBN 978-1-4814-8949-2 • ISBN 978-1-4814-8950-8 (eBook)

For Franny Baucum, who is *nothing* like a frog

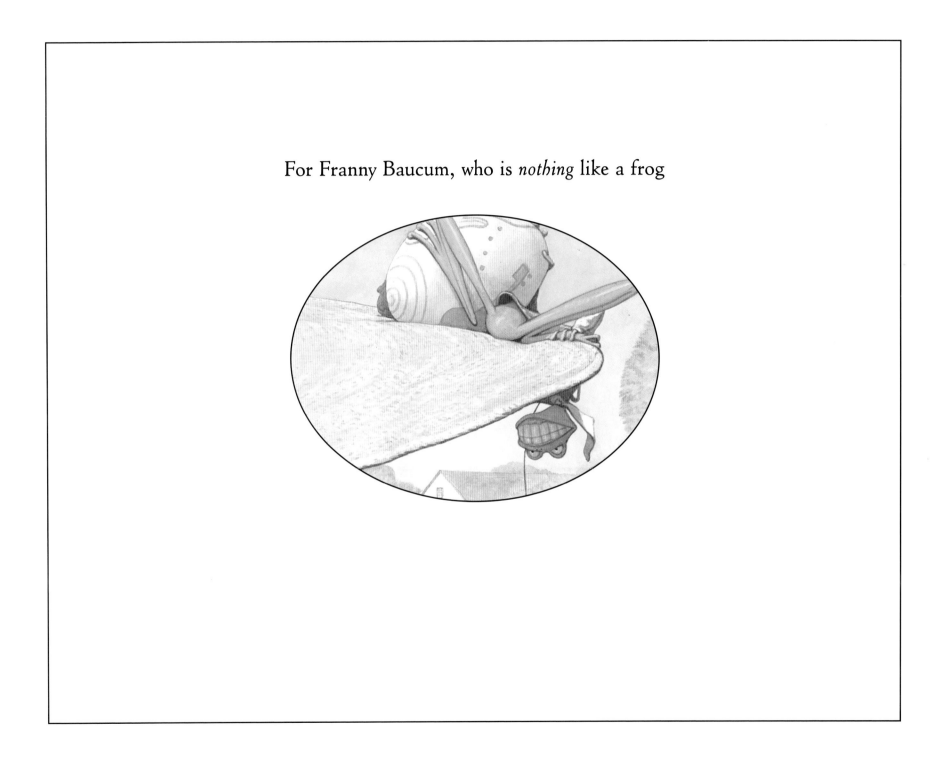

BENTLY HOPPERTON was a rather musical young frog who loved to draw. His best friend was Kack Kack, a recently widowed duck of the wood who lived next door. She made sure Bently's clothes were clean, nursed him when he was sick, and she loved his songs and drawings.

"Oh, sing to me, Bently," she'd say, and happy in the company of his one true friend, Bently would sing his heart out. But one day Kack Kack forgot to ask Bently to sing, and she forgot to look at his drawings. In fact, she forgot Bently altogether. At sunset, Bently went looking for Kack Kack and found her sitting very quietly on her nest.

"Look, Bently!" she said proudly, rising. There, in the middle of the nest, was a single white egg.

"Isn't it beautiful?" asked Kack Kack.

Bently didn't know. *It's just an egg,* he thought.

Kack Kack spent all her time sitting on her beloved egg. Bently felt he hadn't a friend in the world.

One day Kack Kack received a message by cricket courier: Her sister had just hatched seven little ducklings. "Oh, Bently, I must go and see them. Would you please watch over my egg while I'm gone?"

"Well . . . okay," he said.

"Thanks," she quacked, and pecked him on the cheek.

Left alone with the egg, Bently frowned. "Silly old egg," he muttered.

Soon, one wood creature after another scurried by the nest. "We're off to see the new ducklings," they said. "Won't you come with us, Bently?" But Bently shook his head and sat glumly, guarding Kack Kack's solitary egg.

Bently stared at the egg. He didn't know why, but he just didn't like it. It looked bald and bare. It looked dull and pale. It looked so blank. Then he had an idea. He would paint the egg!

He did a beautiful job, a masterful and extraordinary job. The egg looked dazzling. Never in the history of the wood had there been such a special egg.

"Now, this is an egg a frog could get attached to," Bently said proudly, then pulled out his banjo and began to sing.

"Oh, special egg, oh, roundy egg,
Oh, splendid, artful Bently egg,
I painted you with feelings, too,
Mysterious to say to you."

Bently felt happy beyond words.

Suddenly, there was a great rustling. Tree limbs crackled. Shouts echoed. There was a boy in the woods!

Bently tried desperately to hide the egg with straw and leaves, but it was too late.

A hand reached into the nest and roughly grabbed the egg.

"Smash!" said the boy, raising it above his head. But then he looked at its remarkable decoration.

"The Easter Bunny left it," he whispered in awe.

Easter Bunny, my eye, thought Bently. *That's a Bently Hopperton egg!*

The boy cradled the egg carefully and ran away. Bently was beside himself. "Eggnapped!" he cried. "I'll save you, egg. Don't worry, egg. Armed only with my wits, I'll not fail you, egg." And he dashed off in pursuit.

"Oh, please let him be careful with my egg," Bently pleaded as he hopped frantically, trying to keep up. But as he crossed into a garden, he found to his horror that the boy was nowhere in sight.

"I've lost him!" he moaned.

"Me too," sighed a stuffed elephant standing by a row of cabbages. "I've been out here a week! I think he forgot me. I hope it doesn't rain."

"Oh, dear, so do I," Bently said with genuine concern. "Did a boy carrying an extraordinary egg pass by here?"

"Yep," said the elephant. "He turned left at the cucumber squash."

"Thanks so much," Bently said as he dashed away. "Don't worry. I'll try to send you help."

"Appreciate it," said the elephant.

At the cucumber squash, Bently found the boy's tracks and followed them into the house. He had never been in a house before, so he was more than a little afraid.

"I must not falter. The egg is all," he reminded himself to bolster his courage.

Going from room to room, Bently finally spotted the egg.

Using a nearby balloon, Bently floated up to it. Deftly lassoing it, he quickly examined the egg for cracks. It was still perfect! His decoration was perfect too—not even a smudge.

"Oh, joy! Oh, rapture!" he sighed, then broke into song:

"Oh, foundling egg, my captured egg—"

"There's really no time for a serenade, you know," interrupted the watery voice of a nearby goldfish. "He'll be back any second."

"You're right," said Bently, embarrassed. "I just get carried away sometimes!"

"Don't we all," sighed the goldfish.

So, using all his might, Bently loaded the egg into the basket of the balloon, scribbling a message for the boy before he went aloft:

The egg is mine. It needs me. Your elephant is in the garden. It needs you.
Bently Hopperton

"You won't tell him which way we went, will you?" Bently asked the goldfish.

"Cross my gills and hope to drown."

"Thanks," said Bently, steering toward the window.

To Bently's dismay, the balloon instead drifted into the room of a little girl who sat propped up in her bed, painting. She looked a bit like the boy, only nicer.

"Hello there," said the girl. "Do you like my pajamas? They're new."

"Very lovely," replied Bently.

"I'm sick, you know," she sighed. "I'm going to miss the Easter egg hunt today. But that's a nice egg you've got there! A *really* nice egg."

"Why, thank you," said Bently, tightening his grip on the egg. "I'd give it to you, but it belongs to someone else."

The girl bowed her head sadly.

"Look here!" Bently said impatiently, for he thought Kack Kack might be home by now and worrying. "I've got an idea." In a flash, he painted an egg on a piece of paper, which he handed to the little girl. She smiled. The egg matched her pajamas.

Bently hopped back into the balloon, and the little girl, smiling sweetly, gave it a gentle shove.

"Thanks," Bently called as they sailed out the window.

The breeze was steady; the balloon flew straight and true. Never had frog or egg soared so high. Bently was moved to song:

"Oh, flying egg, sky-high-ing egg,
My aeronautic high-up egg,
I look at you as we drift through
The heavens that are bright and—"

But before Bently could finish, there was a loud hissing, and the balloon began to plummet to the ground. Bently looked up. There was a hole in the balloon! Bently looked down. There was an Easter egg hunt just below them. They were headed straight for a lady in a great big hat.

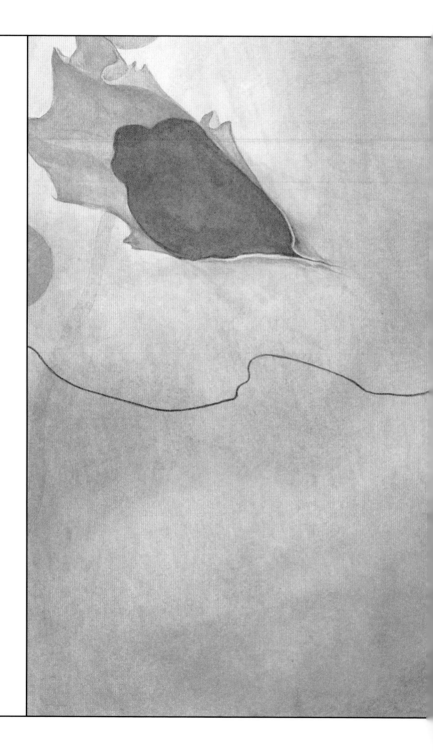

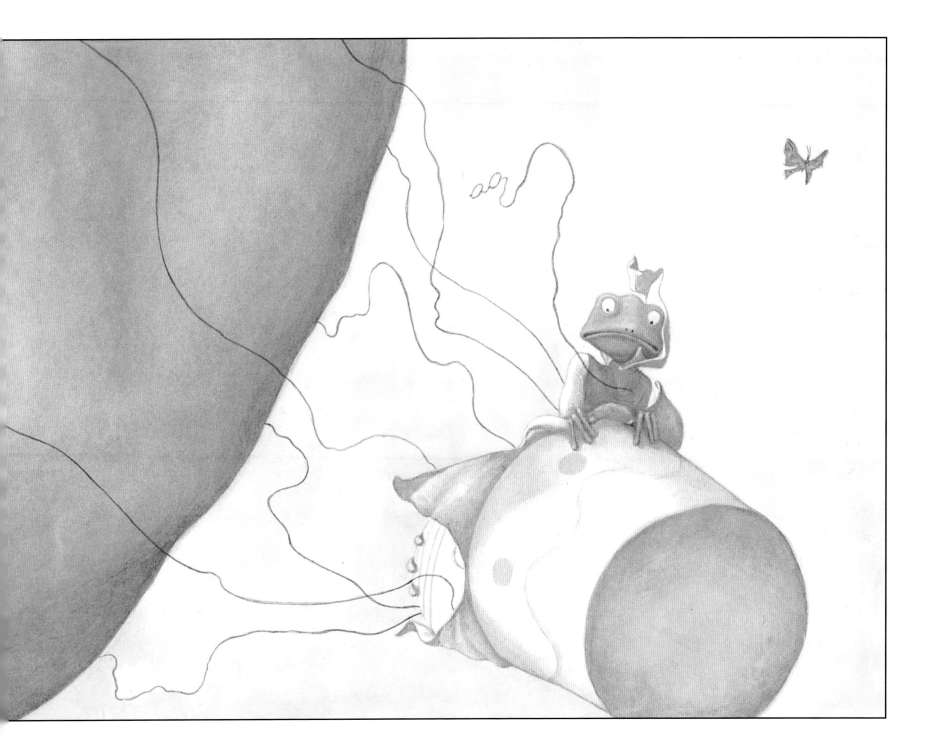

Bently shut his eyes and clutched the egg for dear life. The balloon smacked onto the woman's head, and Bently and the egg spilled out.

"DAPHNE! DAPHNE! There's a frog on your hat!" someone screamed.

Bently grabbed the egg and, trying to look nonchalant, hopped to another woman's hat. The lady next to her began to scream. Everybody began to scream. Food began to fly. There was pandemonium!

Amid all the confusion, Bently and the egg, disguised as hors d'oeuvres, slipped away undetected.

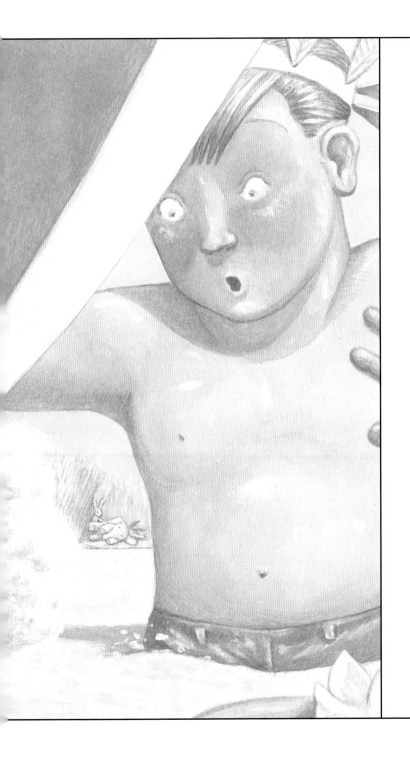

At the bank of a pond, Bently spotted a toy boat. "I'm sure no one would mind if we borrowed this for a bit," he said, panting. Wearily, he loaded the egg onboard and cast off.

"Something of a sea dog, aren't I?" said Bently to the egg, and with a flourish he steered a course across the pond.

The egg sat amidships, shimmering in the afternoon sun. It looked beautiful. Once again Bently was moved to song:

> *"Oh, sailin' egg, mast-mainin' egg,*
> *Our travels have been whirligig.*
> *I sail us to your mother, who*
> *Sits at home and yearns for—"*

But once again events would not let him finish, for wading toward them was the boy.

"I want my egg back," he demanded, and threw a rock, which smashed against the ship's bow.

"I have not yet begun to fight!" Bently proclaimed, and fired the ship's cannons.

The roar of the guns so startled the boy that he ran off crying for his mother.

"Smart bit of sailoring, if I say so myself," Bently said to the egg with some pride. Then he noticed the ship was sinking.

"Yikes!" cried Bently. There was no time to lose. He cut away a line of the ship's rigging, tying one end to his waist and the other around the egg. He swam desperately to shore. The egg was heavy and almost pulled him under several times, but Bently paddled on valiantly. Finally, with his last remaining ounce of strength, Bently plopped the egg upon the shore and whispered hoarsely, "Silly old egg, safe at last." Then he laid down his head and fell into a deep, exhausted sleep.

Bently hadn't noticed, but the egg had been washed clean. All his beautiful decorations were gone. But even if he had noticed, he would no longer have cared, for now he loved the egg just the way it was.

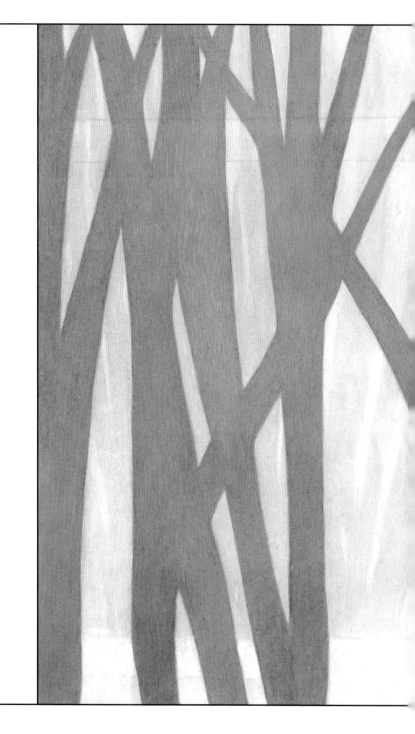

When Bently at last woke up, he blinked and looked over at the egg. His heart sank. It was broken, covered with a dozen tiny cracks.

"Oh no . . . oh no . . ." he moaned.

Then the cracks grew wider and wider, and he heard a tiny sound—the sound only newborn ducklings make. The shell began to crumble, and out wobbled the most beautiful baby duck Bently had ever seen.

Then he saw that Kack Kack was there. "It's a boy! It's a baby boy!" she cried, and gently smoothed the duckling's downy feathers.

Suddenly, there was a great hue and cry. "Hooray for Bently. Long live Bently!" Startled, Bently looked around. It seemed every creature in the wood was there.

"I think I'll name him Ben, after you," said Kack Kack, helping Bently to his feet. "It's the least I can do, after all you've done."

"All I've done? How did you find out?"

"Well, a goldfish told a gnat, and the gnat told some of us," said a turtle.

"And a little girl told a butterfly, and the butterfly told most of us," said a wren.

"And an elephant told a rabbit, and the rabbit told all of us," said a squirrel.

And Kack Kack said, "I'm so proud of you, Bently."

Bently blushed and smiled modestly.

The next afternoon, when everything was quiet again, Kack Kack said, "Oh, sing to us, Bently." And Bently, happy in the company of his two best friends, sang his heart out.

"Oh, happy you, oh, happy me.
The three of us will always be
The best of friends through thick and thin—
Bently, Kack, and little Ben."

And they were all, each one, happy beyond words.

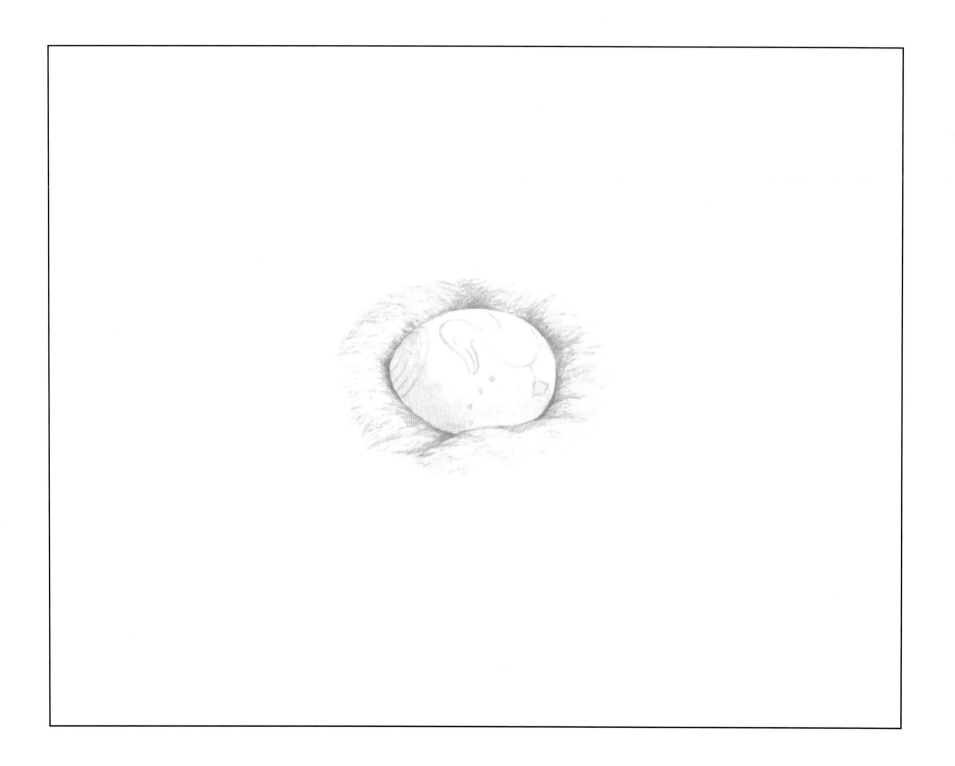